ABOUT THE BANK STREET READY-TO-READ SERIES

Seventy years of educational research and innovative teaching have given the Bank Street College of Education the reputation as America's most trusted name in early childhood education.

Because no two children are exactly alike in their development, we have designed the *Bank Street Ready-to-Read* series in three levels to accommodate the individual stages of reading readiness of children ages four through eight.

- ○ *Level 1:* GETTING READY TO READ—read-alouds for children who are taking their first steps toward reading.

- ● *Level 2:* READING TOGETHER—for children who are just beginning to read by themselves but may need a little help.

- ○ *Level 3:* I CAN READ IT MYSELF—for children who can read independently.

Our three levels make it easy to select the books most appropriate for a child's development and enable him or her to grow with the series step by step. The *Bank Street Ready-to-Read* books also overlap and reinforce each other, further encouraging the reading process.

We feel that making reading fun and enjoyable is the single most important thing that you can do to help children become good readers. And we hope you'll be a part of Bank Street's long tradition of learning through sharing.

The Bank Street College of Education

B. & T.

1

3/94

9.99

To my parents
—B.D.

NEXT TIME I WILL

A Bantam Little Rooster Book/June 1993

Little Rooster is a trademark of Bantam Books,
a division of Bantam Doubleday Dell Publishing Group, Inc.

Series graphic design by Alex Jay/Studio J

Special thanks to James A. Levine, Betsy Gould,
Diane Arico, and Libby Ford.

Library of Congress Cataloging-in-Publication Data

Orgel, Doris.
Next time I will / retold by Doris Orgel;
illustrated by Betsy Day.
p.   cm.—(Bank Street ready-to-read)
"A Byron Preiss book."
"A Bantam Little Rooster book."
Summary: In attempting to follow his mother's instructions,
a good-hearted boy always does the right thing
at the wrong time.
ISBN 0-553-09031-3.—ISBN 0-553-37147-9 (pbk.)
[1. Folklore—England.]   I. Day, Betsy, ill.
II. Title.   III. Series.
PZ8.1.059Ne   1993
398.21—dc20
92-10772   CIP   AC

Published simultaneously in the United States and Canada

PRINTED IN THE UNITED STATES OF AMERICA

0 9 8 7 6 5 4 3 2 1

Next Time I Will

An Old English Tale

Retold by Doris Orgel
Illustrated by Betsy Day

A Byron Preiss Book

A BANTAM LITTLE ROOSTER BOOK

NEW YORK · TORONTO · LONDON · SYDNEY · AUCKLAND

In a humble hut in the woods
lived a good-hearted boy
named Bill.
His mother earned their bread
by spinning yarn.
But it was not enough.

One Monday they ate only
cabbage soup for supper,
and were hungry all night long.

On Tuesday morning Bill said,
"I am old enough now, Mother.
I will go out and find work."

So he put on his shabby coat
and set out.
On his way he passed
a fine, big house on a hill.
"Who lives there?" he wondered.

A rich man lived there
with his daughter, Sally.
Sally was a sad girl
who never spoke.
She never laughed or even smiled.
Her father called in many doctors.
They tried many medicines.
But it was no use.

Bill passed the rich man's house
and soon found work on a farm.
He worked cheerfully all day,
and the farmer paid him a penny.

The penny gleamed in his hand.
Bill was happy and proud.

10

But on his way home
the penny fell into a brook.

"Silly Bill," said his mother.
"Why didn't you put it
in your pocket?"
"Next time I will," said Bill.

The next day Bill worked
in a cow barn.
He milked the cows and got paid
a jar of good fresh milk.
He put the jar in his pocket.
But the pocket ripped and
out spilled the milk.

When he got home,
not a drop was left.
"What a pity," said his mother.
"Why didn't you carry it
on your head?"
"Next time I will," said Bill.

The next day Bill herded goats.
He got paid a soft, smelly cheese.
He carried it home on his head,
but it melted.

16

It stuck to his hair in clumps.
It ran down his face and neck.
"Ugh, what a mess!"
cried his mother.
"Why didn't you carry it
in your hands?"
And Bill said, "Next time I will."

On Friday Bill worked for a baker.
The baker was poor himself.
All he could give Bill for pay
was a big old cat.
Bill tried to carry it in his hands,
but the cat wiggled so much
Bill had to let it go.

He came home with nothing
but scratches.
"How foolish!" cried his mother.
"Why didn't you tie it
with a string and pull it?"
"Next time I will," said Bill.

20

On Saturday he worked
for a butcher.
The butcher gave Bill
a good piece of meat.
Bill tied it with a string
and pulled it home
through muck and mud.

"You numbskull!" cried his mother.
"Now we have no Sunday dinner!
Why didn't you carry it
on your shoulder?"
And Bill said, "Next time I will."

Bill felt very bad.
He wanted to make up for it.
So he worked the next day,
even though it was Sunday.
This time his pay was
a good gray donkey.

Poor Bill!
He had a hard time
lifting that donkey
onto his shoulders.
But at last he did it
and struggled home.

Silent Sally and her father
looked out the window.
Sally was as sad as ever.
Then she saw Bill climb the hill
with the donkey around his neck.
The donkey's hind legs
dangled down.
His front legs danced in the air.
His tail swung to and fro.
"Eee aww, eee aww!" he brayed.

And do you know what happened?

Sally started smiling—yes!
Then she laughed.
Then she spoke.
"Who is that funny fellow?"
said Sally, loud and clear.
"You spoke!" her father cried.

28

He rushed outside to Bill.
"You made my daughter speak
and laugh—at last!
Tell me, how can we thank you?"

Bill ran home, all excited.
"Mother, put on your Sunday dress!"
"What for?" she sighed.
"We have no Sunday dinner."
But Bill said, "Just come with me!"

He took her to the house on the hill.
They had a wonderful dinner:
fresh ham and sweet potato pie.

"Come back every Sunday,"
said Sally and her father.
Then they gave Bill and
his mother a special parting gift:
a great basket filled
with good things to eat.

31

"Mother, are you pleased now?"
asked Bill.
"Yes, very pleased," she replied.
"For you have a kind heart,
dear Bill,
and can make people laugh.
Those are the best gifts of all."